The WIZARD of OZ

hinkler

hinkler

Published by Hinkler Books Pty Ltd
45–55 Fairchild Street
Heatherton Victoria 3202 Australia
www.hinkler.com

© Hinkler Books Pty Ltd 2003, 2016, 2019

Abridged adaptation written by Archie Oliver
Original story written by L. Frank Baum
Cover illustration: Laura Stitzel
Illustrations: Geraldine Rodriguez and Brijbasi Art Press
Typesetting: Ben Galpin
Prepress: Splitting Image

ISBN: 978 1 4889 3861 0

Printed and bound in China

The WIZARD OF OZ

L. FRANK BAUM

The Author

L. Frank Baum (1856–1919)

American writer Lyman Frank Baum created the strange and magical world of the Land of Oz in bedtime stories he told his children. They loved his stories so much that he started to write them down.

In 1900 he published *The Wonderful Wizard of Oz*. It was a huge success. Baum went on to write 13 other books about the Land of Oz.

The Wonderful Wizard of Oz was the most successful. It has been an international best-seller for more than one hundred years. The 1939 film, *The Wizard of Oz*, based on the book and starring Judy Garland, is an all-time box office hit.

Baum, born in Chittenango, New York, was the son of an oil magnate. Before he became a full-time writer, his jobs included running a store, chicken farming and journalism.

Contents

Chapter 1

The Great Wind

Dorothy stood on the porch and looked anxiously out across the prairie. A great wind howled ever closer to the little wooden house, where she lived with Uncle Henry, Aunt Em and Toto, her little black dog.

The wind whipped up a dust storm and as it raced towards her, the house began to shake and shudder.

Dorothy was worried. Uncle Henry and

Aunt Em were both still out working in the fields and were nowhere to be seen. Toto began to whine, so she wrapped her arms around him.

Suddenly, the great wind hit the little house.

With the front door still open, the house began to fill with wind. In seconds, it seemed as if all the walls would be blown out. But instead, Dorothy felt the house lift off from its foundations and whirl up into the sky.

It grew dark and cold. It was as if Dorothy, Toto and the house had been wrapped up in a great black swirling cloud.

Dorothy gripped Toto with one arm. Toto did not like the wind and he barked very loudly.

Hour after hour passed and, very gradually, Dorothy got used to the feeling of the house whirling around in the darkness. She wondered if the house would ever come back down to earth again.

Then, the strangest thing happened. She closed her eyes and fell asleep.

Dorothy awoke to find Toto licking her face.

She was lying on the floor of the kitchen in the little house, and all was quiet. The house was not moving anymore and sunshine flooded in through the front windows.

Dorothy sprang to her feet. With Toto at her heels, she ran to the front door and looked out.

The little girl let out a cry of amazement. The wind had set the house down in a lush green meadow. Around it, there were huge trees groaning under the weight of ripe fruit.

A babbling brook ran past close by, its banks

covered with the most beautiful flowers. Flocks of strange, exotic birds were drinking from the brook.

Dorothy noticed a group of very strange people approaching the house.

At first Dorothy thought they were children. But as they got closer, she realised that there were men, women and children amongst the group – but they were all Dorothy's height. They were all dressed completely in blue. Even their long boots were blue, and some wore little hats that were tall and pointy, with tinkling bells around the rims.

There was also a tall woman among the group. She wore a large crown and she carried a long magical-looking wand that had a silver star atop it. She was wearing a beautiful gown covered in little stars, which glistened in the sun like diamonds. Her face was kind.

The woman walked up to Dorothy and bowed. 'Most noble sorceress, welcome to the Land of Oz,' she began. 'We are so grateful to you for killing the Wicked Witch of the East.

You have set the Munchkins free at last.'

Dorothy scratched her head. What on earth was this woman talking about? And who were the Munchkins?

Chapter 2

The Munchkins

'There must be some mistake,' Dorothy said, staring at the strange woman. 'I have never met anyone called the Wicked Witch of the East. And I certainly haven't killed her!'

'Your house killed her then,' the woman replied, with a laugh. 'See, look there!'

Dorothy gave a cry of fright as she looked down where the woman was pointing and saw two feet sticking out from beneath the house.

Upon the feet were red shoes, with pointed toes.

'Oh, dear! Oh, dear!' cried Dorothy. 'The house must have fallen on her. What can we do?'

'There is nothing to be done,' said the woman calmly. 'She is dead.'

'But who was she?' asked Dorothy.

'She was the Wicked Witch of the East, just as I said,' answered the woman. 'For years she kept the Munchkins as her slaves. They worked for her night and day. Now she's dead, they're free. And that's why they are grateful to you.'

'Who are the Munchkins?' asked Dorothy.

'They are the people who live in the Land of the East, where the Wicked Witch ruled,' the woman replied, gesturing to the people around her who were wearing blue.

'Are you a Munchkin?' said Dorothy.

'No, but I am a friend. When the Munchkins saw that the Witch of the East was dead, they sent for me. I am the Witch of the North.'

'Oh, gracious me!' cried Dorothy. 'Are you a real witch?'

'Yes indeed, but I am a good witch and the people love me. I'm not as powerful as the wicked witch who ruled here. If I had been, I would have set the people free myself.'

Dorothy was a little frightened of facing a real witch. She said she thought that all witches were wicked.

'Oh, no, it is a great mistake to think that,' said the Witch of the North.

She explained that there had been four witches in the Land of Oz. The two who lived in the North and South were good witches, she said.

'That must be true,' she continued, 'because I am the Witch of the North and I know I am good. But the Witch of the East was wicked. So now you have killed her, there is only one wicked witch left in the Land of Oz . . . the Witch of the West.'

'I thought witches only lived in fairy tales,' said Dorothy.

'No! No!' answered the witch. 'We have both

witches and wizards here in the Land of Oz. Oz himself is the Great Wizard. He is more powerful than all the rest of us put together. He lives in the Emerald City.'

Dorothy was going to ask another question when she suddenly pointed to where the feet of the Wicked Witch had been lying. 'Look, the feet have gone!' she cried.

'It is not surprising,' said the Witch of the North. 'She was so old. Her bones must have dried up quickly in the sun and turned to dust. But the shoes are still there. You must have them to wear.'

The witch explained that she knew the shoes were blessed with a very powerful charm. 'We know they are charmed,' she said, 'but none of us knows what that charm is. Perhaps you will find out one day.'

'All I want is to find my way back to my Aunt Em and Uncle Henry in Kansas,' replied Dorothy. 'Can you show me the way home?'

The Munchkins looked at each other in confusion and shook their heads.

'The Land of the East is all desert,' said one.

'So is the South,' said a second. 'That's where the Quadlings live.'

'The Land of the West is also all desert,' said a third. 'That's the home of the Winkies, and the Wicked Witch of the West.'

'The North is my home,' said the Witch, 'so why don't you come and live with me?'

Dorothy began to cry. She suddenly felt very alone, with no hope of getting back home again.

Chapter 3

A Message from the Wizards

Dorothy's tears made the Munchkins feel very sorry for her. They immediately took out their handkerchiefs and started to weep too.

The Witch of the North didn't cry, but took action straight away. She took off her jewelled crown, balanced it on the end of her nose and counted: 'One. Two. Three!'

The witch's crown suddenly changed into a small blackboard with eight words printed on it, in chalk:

Dorothy, you must go to the Emerald City.

'Oh!' cried the Witch in delight. 'Your name must be Dorothy. This is a message from the wizards telling you to go to the Emerald City. That's where you'll find a way back to Kansas.'

'Where is the Emerald City?' asked Dorothy.

'It is exactly in the centre of the country. It's where Oz, the Great Wizard, lives.'

'Is he a good man?' inquired the little girl anxiously.

'He is a good wizard,' said the witch. 'Whether he is a man or not, I cannot tell. I have never seen him.'

Dorothy asked how she could reach the city.

'You must walk there. It is a dangerous journey. But I will use all my magic skills to keep you from harm.'

'Won't you come with me?' begged Dorothy, who was beginning to see the Witch of the North as her only friend in this strange new world.

'I cannot,' she answered, 'but I will give you a kiss. No one would dare hurt someone who had been kissed by the Witch of the North.'

The witch kissed Dorothy gently on the forehead. A small, shiny mark appeared where her lips had touched.

'The road to the Emerald City,' she continued, pointing her wand in the direction Dorothy was to go, 'is paved with yellow brick. So you cannot miss it. And if you see the Wizard of Oz, don't be afraid of him. Just tell him your story and ask him to help. Now goodbye, my dear.'

The Munchkins bowed to Dorothy, wished her a pleasant journey and walked off into the woods.

The Witch of the North gave Dorothy a friendly nod, whirled around on her heels three times, and vanished.

Toto growled at the spot where the witch had been standing.

Dorothy walked back into the house and filled a basket with some bread. Then she tried on the shoes that had belonged to the Wicked Witch of the East. They fit perfectly.

'Come on Toto,' she cried. 'Let's go to the Emerald City and ask the Great Wizard of Oz how to get back to Kansas!'

It didn't take Dorothy long to find the yellow brick road. Soon she and Toto were on their way.

The sun shone brightly and all the birds were singing. You might imagine that Dorothy felt miserable after being suddenly whisked away from her own country, and set down in a foreign land.

But she didn't mind quite so much now. She felt quite happy as she walked along the yellow brick road.

When evening came, Dorothy looked around for a place to spend the night. She saw a group of Munchkins, who were dancing in a field beside a beautiful little house.

They were celebrating their freedom from the slavery of the Wicked Witch of the East. They had already been told that it was Dorothy who had killed the witch, so there was nothing they wouldn't do for her.

She ate a hearty supper with them and then had a good night's sleep. In the morning, she had a huge breakfast. Then she and Toto set off on the yellow brick road again.

Dorothy hadn't gone far when she noticed a scarecrow on the edge of a cornfield.

She paused on the road and gazed at the scarecrow. Its head was made of a small sack, stuffed with straw. A nose, two eyes and a mouth had been painted on it. An old straw hat was perched on its head.

The scarecrow was wearing a faded suit and old boots. Every piece of clothing had also been stuffed with straw. It was standing high up above the corn stalks, supported by a pole stuck up its back.

Dorothy was about to walk on when she suddenly saw the scarecrow wink at her. She shrieked with surprise!

Chapter 4

The Scarecrow

'Good day,' said the Scarecrow, in a husky voice.

Dorothy was astonished. Scarecrows in Kansas didn't wink, let alone talk.

'Did you speak?' she asked, in wonder.

'Certainly,' answered the Scarecrow. 'How do you do?'

'I'm pretty well, thank you,' replied Dorothy politely. 'How do you do?'

'I'm not too good just now,' he replied, 'because it gets very boring being perched up here day and night, to scare away the crows.'

'Can't you get down?' asked Dorothy.

'No. I've got a pole stuck up my back. Can you help me off?'

Dorothy reached up and lifted the scarecrow off the pole. Being stuffed with straw, he wasn't very heavy at all.

'Thanks,' he said. 'I feel like a new scarecrow already. Now tell me where you are going.'

'I'm going to the Emerald City to see the Wizard of Oz,' she answered.

'And where is Emerald City and who is the Wizard of Oz?'

'Don't you know?' asked Dorothy.

'Of course I don't know,' said the Scarecrow. 'I don't know anything. I'm stuffed with straw. I have no brains at all.'

'Oh,' said Dorothy, 'I'm awfully sorry for you.'

'Do you think,' asked the Scarecrow, 'that if I went to the Emerald City, the Wizard could give me some brains?'

'I don't know,' replied Dorothy. 'But you can come with me. If Oz can't give you any brains, you won't be any worse off than you are now.'

'I don't mind my legs, arms and body being stuffed with straw,' said the Scarecrow. 'If anyone treads on my toes or sticks a pin into me it doesn't hurt. I can't feel it. But I don't want people to think I am a fool.'

Dorothy said she understood how he felt. 'I'll ask Oz to do everything he can.'

And so Dorothy, Toto and the Scarecrow set off on the yellow brick road. The strange creature looked a little nervous as Toto sniffed at his heels. Dorothy told him not to worry because Toto never bit anyone.

'I'm not afraid of dogs,' said the Scarecrow. 'There's only one thing I'm really afraid of. And that's someone lighting a match close to me and setting me on fire!'

After a while, Dorothy became hungry and took out some bread from her basket. She offered some to the Scarecrow.

'Thank you, but I am never hungry,' he said. 'My mouth is only painted on.'

Soon they entered a dark forest. To pass the time, Dorothy asked the Scarecrow about his life.

'There's nothing to tell,' he explained. 'I was only made the day before yesterday. All I know is that I was made by the farmer and then put in the field. I felt very alone. Sometimes birds did fly into the field, but as soon as they saw me, they flew off again.'

Dorothy, Toto and the Scarecrow walked until it was nearly dark. Eventually, Dorothy spotted a small cottage just off the road.

The cottage was empty, so Dorothy went inside. She saw a bed of dried leaves in one corner. Dorothy was so tired that she lay down and instantly fell asleep. Toto slept beside her. The Scarecrow, of course, was never tired.

He stood in a corner, patiently waiting for morning to come.

When Dorothy awoke the sun was shining again. Toto was already outside chasing the birds, and the Scarecrow was still standing in the corner.

'I must find some water to drink,' said Dorothy.

So they both went outside and looked around. They hadn't gone far when Dorothy heard a deep groan.

'What was that?' she asked timidly.

'I cannot imagine,' said the Scarecrow. 'Let's go and see.'

They walked into the forest, in the direction of the noise. Suddenly, Dorothy saw a huge tree that had been cut down. And standing beside it, with a raised axe in his hands, was a man made entirely of tin!

Chapter 5

The Tin Man

The Tin Man stood perfectly motionless. Even his axe was frozen in mid-air.

Toto ran up and snapped at the Tin Man's leg. The little dog could not have been more surprised. The tin leg almost broke Toto's teeth! And then Dorothy heard the strangest sound.

'Did you groan?' asked Dorothy, hardly expecting this strange metal man to hear anything.

'Yes,' answered the Tin Man. 'I did. I've been groaning for more than a year, ever since I came out here to cut down some trees for firewood. Then it rained and all my joints rusted up. I can't move.'

Dorothy asked what she could do for him. 'Get an oilcan and oil my joints,' he answered. 'They are rusted so badly. You'll find an oilcan in my cottage.'

Dorothy suddenly realised that it was the Tin Man's cottage in which they had spent the night. She hurried back and returned with the oilcan.

'My neck first, please,' begged the Tin Man.

One squeeze of oil and the Tin Man moved his head again.

'Now the arms and legs,' he said.

It wasn't long before the Tin Man could move his whole body. 'Oh, you can't imagine,' he said, 'how nice it is to move again. I might have stood here forever if you hadn't come along. Where are you going?'

Dorothy explained that she was on her way to see the Wizard of Oz, to see if he could help her to get back home to Kansas.

'The Scarecrow is coming with me because he wants the Wizard to give him a brain.'

The Tin Man was very interested. 'If I came with you,' he asked, 'do you think Oz could give me a heart?'

'I expect he could,' said Dorothy. 'If he can find the Scarecrow a brain, I don't see why he couldn't give you a heart.'

So the Tin Man put his axe over his shoulder and joined Dorothy, the Scarecrow and Toto on the yellow brick road.

'Keep the oilcan in your basket,' he suggested. 'You never know when it might rain. I don't want to be rusted up again!'

While they walked, the Tin Man told his story.

***

'I am the son of a woodman,' he began, 'and I fell in love with a Munchkin girl. But her mother didn't want her to marry me, so she asked a wicked witch to enchant my axe. Soon after, I slipped while chopping wood and the axe cut off my left leg.

'I went to a blacksmith who made me a tin leg, and I started work again. The leg worked well, but the witch saw it and enchanted my axe again. I tried to hold it firmly in my hands, but I couldn't control it. This time it cut off my right leg.

'I got the man to make me another tin leg. This annoyed the witch even more. After this, the enchanted axe cut off both my arms. The man gave me two tin ones. Then the old witch made the axe slip and cut off my head. I thought this was the end, but the man made me a new head out of tin.

'I thought I had beaten the wicked witch, but then she made the axe cut me in half. Once more the man put me together, with a tin body. It was marvellous, but the one thing the man could not make me was a tin heart. Without a heart, I could not love my little Munchkin girl. So I lost her.'

***

Dorothy felt so sorry for the Tin Man.

'I do hope the Wizard of Oz can give me a heart,' he said. 'Oh, if I had a heart I could go back and ask the Munchkin girl to marry me.'

'I'd rather have a brain than a heart,' said the Scarecrow, 'because a fool like me would not know what to do with a heart, even if he had one.'

The Tin Man smiled. 'I'll ask Oz for a heart,' he said, 'because brains can't make a man happy.

But a heart can make you happy, and happiness is the best thing in the world.'

Dorothy wasn't sure who was right. She decided that if only she could get back to Kansas and Aunty Em, it wouldn't matter so much who had a brain and who had a heart.

Dorothy, Toto, the Scarecrow and the Tin Man were still walking in the forest, and it was getting darker all the time.

'How long will it be,' asked Dorothy, 'before we are out of this forest?'

'I don't know,' answered the Tin Man. 'My father came this way once and he told me that the forest was the most dangerous part of the way to the Emerald City. He said it was full of wild beasts.'

Just as he spoke, a terrible roar came from the forest. The next moment, a great Lion bounded into the road in front of them.

With one blow of his paw, he sent the Scarecrow spinning into the air. Then he knocked down the Tin Man, too.

Toto ran towards the Lion. The noble beast reared up with a roar, ready to swipe Toto! But just as he did, the Scarecrow threw himself forward to protect the little dog – and was struck down by one of the lion's great paws. The Lion then turned back to Toto, his great gaping mouth ready to bite!

Chapter 6

The Cowardly Lion

'Don't you dare eat my dog!' screamed Dorothy, leaping forward and punching the Lion on the nose. 'You should be ashamed of yourself, a big beast like you trying to eat a little dog like Toto!'

The Lion's jaws snapped shut.

'I didn't want to bite him,' said the creature, rubbing his sore nose with a paw.

'No, but you tried to,' answered Dorothy. 'You are nothing but a big coward!'

'I know it,' whimpered the Lion. 'I've always known it. But I can't help it.'

Dorothy wasn't finished with him yet. 'To think, you struck a stuffed man like the Scarecrow.'

'Is he stuffed?' asked the surprised Lion.

'Of course he's stuffed. He's a scarecrow!' replied Dorothy.

'So that's why he fell over so easily,' remarked the Lion. 'Is the other one stuffed too?'

'No!' said Dorothy, who was still angry. 'He's made of tin.'

'Is the little one stuffed or made of tin?' said the Lion, pointing with his paw at Toto.

'No,' said Dorothy. 'He's a dog. He's made of flesh and bone, like you and I. Now tell me why you are such a coward!'

'It's a mystery to me,' replied the Lion. 'All the animals in the forest expect me to be brave. They tell me the Lion is the King of the Forest. But I'm not. I just roar very loudly when I'm scared and every creature runs away from me.'

'That isn't right,' said Dorothy. 'The King of the Forest shouldn't be a coward.'

Just then, the Scarecrow interrupted. 'Perhaps the Wizard of Oz could give the Lion some courage.'

'Do you think Oz could give me courage?' asked the Lion excitedly. 'I shall never be happy until I am brave.'

'I don't see why not,' said Dorothy. 'And besides, even though you are not brave yet, your roar will keep the wild beasts away from us on our journey.'

So the little group set off down the yellow brick road once more, the Lion walking proudly at Dorothy's side.

That night, they camped under a big tree in the forest. The Tin Man chopped some wood for their fire. The Scarecrow kept his distance, as he didn't want to set fire to himself.

Dorothy and Toto shared a meal of the bread that remained in Dorothy's basket. The Lion headed off into the forest to hunt for his food.

Soon after they heard a shriek, and later the Lion returned with a very full stomach. Nobody wanted to know what the Lion had caught and eaten!

They set off early the next morning, but soon found their way blocked by a huge ditch that lay right across the yellow brick road.

They crept up to the edge and peered down. It was very deep, with sharp jagged rocks at the bottom. The sides were so steep that no one could have climbed down, and up the other side.

'What shall we do?' asked Dorothy.

The Tin Man said he hadn't the faintest idea. The Scarecrow said they couldn't fly across.

But the Lion thought he might be able to leap across it.

'And you can carry us on your back, one at a time,' said Dorothy.

It was agreed, although the Lion was thinking he might not be brave enough to make the jump.

The Scarecrow was the lightest, so he climbed onto the Lion's back first. He was shaking with fear. So was the Lion.

Chapter 7

The Kalidahs

The Lion walked to the edge of the terrifying chasm and crouched down.

'Why don't you run and jump?' asked the Scarecrow.

'Because,' said the Lion proudly, 'that isn't the way we lions do these things.'

Then, giving a great spring, the Lion shot into the air with the Scarecrow holding on to his neck. They landed safely on the other side.

Dorothy and Toto were next. Once more the Lion made a successful leap. The Tin Man went last.

After resting for a while, they set off down the road again. They walked all day. As evening fell, it began to grow dark. Strange noises were coming from the depths of the forest.

'It must be the Kalidahs,' whispered the Lion, who was shaking with fear again.

'What are the Kalidahs?' asked Dorothy.

'Huge beasts, with bodies like bears and heads like tigers,' said the Lion. 'They've claws so long and sharp, they could tear me in two.'

They all started walking faster, but very soon they came upon another huge ditch crossing the yellow brick road. This one was much wider and deeper than the first. There was no way the Lion could jump across it.

On the other side of the ditch, there were remains of a broken bridge that had once joined the two sides together. This gave the Tin Man an idea. With his sharp axe, he chopped down a huge tree near the ditch. It crashed down across the ditch and its trunk reached from the side they now stood to the broken-off bridge on the other side.

'See!' said the Tin Man. 'Now we can use the tree as a bridge.'

They had just started to cross the bridge when they heard a series of howls and growls. They looked back. To their horror, they saw some huge beasts running towards them.

'It's the Kalidahs!' cried the Lion.

Dorothy and the others ran across the tree

trunk. As they reached the other side, the Kalidahs were about to leap onto the tree too. Then the Lion turned and opened his mouth wide. His terrifying teeth glinted, as he let out the most enormous roar.

The Kalidahs were so surprised at the noise that they stopped in their tracks. Now the Tin Man started hacking at the tree trunk with his axe.

The Kalidahs saw what the Tin Man was doing and rushed onto the tree bridge. They were almost across it when he finally cut through the trunk of the tree.

The tree, with several Kalidahs clinging on for grim life, crashed into the gulf far below. The snarling brutes were dashed to pieces on the sharp rocks at the bottom.

'Well, well,' said the cowardly Lion, 'it seems we are all going to live a little longer after all. I've never known my heart beat so fast.'

'I wish I had a heart to beat,' said the Tin Man.

The travellers set off again. Gradually, the forest got lighter and the trees started to thin out.

At last they emerged from the forest and came to a fast-flowing river. They could all see where the yellow brick road continued on the other side of the river. But there was not a bridge to be seen.

'How shall we cross the river?' asked Dorothy.

'We can build a raft!' cried the Scarecrow. 'That will carry us across.'

The Tin Man was soon at work with his axe again. It was a big job, but the raft was finished that night.

They decided to get a good night's sleep before attempting to cross the river in the morning.

Dorothy dreamed of the Emerald City, and of the Wizard of Oz, who would soon show her the way back home.

In the morning they launched the raft. It floated perfectly. Dorothy and Toto went on board first and sat down in the middle. The Lion crept nervously to one end. The Scarecrow and the Tin Man, who each carried a long pole to steer with, stood at the other end.

'Are we all ready?' asked the Tin Man. Everyone said they were.

The Tin Man and the Scarecrow pushed off. The raft slowly left the bank. For a few moments, all went well. But the further into the river they went, the faster the current pushed them.

Soon the raft was out of control and racing away down the river!

Chapter 8

The Field of Sleep

The river current swept the raft downstream, further and further away from the yellow brick road.

The Tin Man and the Scarecrow desperately tried to steer with their poles. But soon the water was so deep that their poles could hardly reach the bottom of the river.

'We're in trouble!' cried the Tin Man. 'The current is carrying us towards the country of the

Wicked Witch of the West. We'll all end up as her slaves.'

'And then I'll get no brains,' said the Scarecrow.

'And I'll get no courage,' said the Lion.

'And I'll get no heart,' said the Tin Man.

'And I'll never get home to Kansas,' said Dorothy.

The Scarecrow was so desperate to turn the boat around that he leant over the side of the raft and pushed his long pole into the bottom of the river.

He pushed the pole so hard that it became stuck fast in the mud. Before he could pull it out again, or let go, the raft was swept away.

The poor Scarecrow was left clinging to the pole in the middle of the river!

'Goodbye!' he called after them, sadly. 'I'll never get a brain now. I'm worse off now than when I was stuck on a pole in the middle of a field. What use is a Scarecrow stuck on a pole in the middle of a river?'

The others were so miserable to see the figure of the Scarecrow becoming smaller and smaller, as the raft was swept further away. The Tin Man felt like crying but then he remembered that his tears might make him rust up again.

Then, the Lion had an idea. 'I could swim and pull the raft after me if one of you holds onto my tail.'

The Lion dived into the water. The Tin Man caught hold of his tail.

It was hard work at first, but the Lion successfully dragged the raft back to the riverbank.

'We must try and get back along the bank to the yellow brick road,' said Dorothy. 'We might even be able to rescue the Scarecrow.'

So they set off along the bank.

Later that morning, a large stork flew by and asked them what they were doing. Dorothy explained that they were trying to find their friend the Scarecrow, and get back to the yellow brick road.

'Your friend is still in the middle of the river. I saw him just now,' said the stork. 'I would have picked him up, but he's probably too big and heavy for me.'

'He's only made of straw,' cried Dorothy. 'He doesn't weigh anything at all.'

'Oh, I see,' said the stork. 'In that case, I'll go and get him.'

A few minutes later, the stork returned with the Scarecrow hanging from his legs.

The Scarecrow was so glad to be back among his friends. He hugged them all.

He turned to the stork. 'Thank you,' he said. 'If I ever get some brains, I'll come back and find you again, and do you a favour too.'

'That's all right,' said the stork, flying off. 'I always like to help someone in trouble.'

Dorothy led them away down the bank. They didn't stop until they came upon a field of brilliant red flowers.

'Aren't they beautiful?' she said.

Dorothy didn't know that these particular flowers had a powerful fragrance. The fragrance could put people to sleep forever, if they weren't rescued within a short time.

Dorothy, Toto and the Lion all ran into the field. And, oh dear, they were all soon fast asleep!

The Tin Man and the Scarecrow, of course, were not made of flesh and blood, so the red flowers had no power over them.

'What shall we do?' asked the Tin Man, when they found they couldn't wake up the three sleepers.

'If we leave them here, they'll never wake up,' said the Tin Man.

'We can carry Dorothy and Toto out,' said the Scarecrow, 'but the Lion is too heavy for us to move.'

'We'll have to leave him behind,' said the Tin Man sadly. 'He will have to sleep forever. Perhaps he will dream that he found his courage at last.'

'I'm sorry,' said the Scarecrow. 'The Lion was a good comrade, even if he was a coward.'

They carried Dorothy and Toto out of the field, and then waited for them to wake up again. As they waited, they suddenly heard a high-pitched squeak and a growl.

The Scarecrow looked around and saw a great yellow wildcat running towards them. Its mouth was open, revealing two rows of razor-sharp teeth. Its eyes glowed like balls of fire.

Just ahead of the wildcat raced a tiny grey field mouse. The wildcat was about to catch the poor mouse and eat it!

Chapter 9

The Queen of the Field Mice

The Tin Man did not have a heart, but he knew it was a cruel thing to kill such a pretty, harmless animal as a field mouse.

He raised his axe and as the wildcat ran past, he cut off the very end of its tail. The animal roared, turned around and ran off in shock.

The field mouse stopped and came back to thank the Tin Man for saving its life.

'Oh, it's nothing,' said the Tin Man. 'Don't

speak of it, I beg you. I like to help those who may need a friend, even if it is only a mouse.'

'Only a mouse!' cried the little creature. 'Why, I am a Queen. I am the Queen of the Field Mice!'

'Oh, I'm sorry,' said the Tin Man, bowing down to the mouse.

'You have done a great deed in saving my life,' she said.

Just then, several other field mice appeared.

'Oh, Your Majesty, we thought you'd been killed by the wildcat!' they said.

As they spoke, they all bowed down to their Queen. They bowed so low they almost stood on their heads.

The Queen of the Field Mice told them how the Tin Man had saved her. 'His reward,' she said, 'will be that you must all serve him and obey his every wish.'

'We will!' cried all the mice at once.

One of the mice asked the Tin Man if there was anything they could do for him.

'There is only one thing,' he replied. 'Could you save our friend, the Lion? He is asleep in the field of red flowers.'

'A Lion!' cried the Queen. 'He would eat us all up!'

'Oh, no,' explained Tin Man. 'The Lion is a coward. He wouldn't hurt anyone.'

'Well, we shall trust your word,' answered the Queen.

Together, they decided that the Tin Man and the Scarecrow would build a wooden cart to carry the Lion. The field mice would then pull it. 'Are you sure you have enough mice to pull the Lion?' asked the Scarecrow. 'He is very heavy.'

'Don't worry about that,' said the Queen. 'You'll see.'

The Queen gave orders for one of the mice

to go and bring the others. 'And don't forget to bring lots of string with you,' she added.

The Scarecrow and the Tin Man went to work. It didn't take them long to build a frame of thick branches to carry the Lion. They fastened it with wooden pegs and cut four circular logs for the wheels.

They had just finished when they saw the most amazing sight. Coming towards them were thousands and thousands of field mice! Each one carried a piece of string.

Just then, Dorothy and Toto awoke. Dorothy was astonished to find herself surrounded by a great army of mice.

'Permit me to introduce Her Majesty, the Queen of the Field Mice,' said the Scarecrow proudly.

Dorothy got to her feet and curtsied to the Queen. They quickly became friends and chatted away, while the mice tied themselves to the wooden cart.

The cart was so much bigger than any of the mice. But it was quite easy to pull with thousands of mice tied to it.

They soon found the sleeping Lion. The mice, with the help of the Scarecrow and the Tin Man, managed to roll him onto the cart and haul him out of the field before they all fell asleep.

Dorothy was so happy to see the Lion. She was glad her friend had been rescued.

Soon after, the mice left. 'Don't forget,' said the Queen, 'if ever you need us again, just call out. We'll hear you, wherever you are.'

It was several hours before the Lion finally awoke. He yawned, stretched himself and got up. 'Oh, that was a good sleep,' he said, 'it's time we got going again.'

He hardly believed it when the others told him all that had happened since he fell asleep. 'Mice could never have pulled me,' he roared. 'You're making it all up!'

They all laughed as they headed back along the bank, and found the yellow brick road again.

The dangers of the river and the dark forest were behind them now. And soon after, they looked down from the top of a hill and saw a marvellous sight.

Below lay a land covered with green-painted houses.

Chapter 10

The Guardian of the Gates

Dorothy and her friends descended into the land and looked for a place to stay the night.

They knocked at the door of the first house they came to. A woman answered it.

'We're looking for somewhere to stay,' said Dorothy.

The woman raised her eyebrows on seeing such a strange group of people and animals. But she said they could stay with her.

'Where are you all going?' she inquired.

'To the Emerald City to see the Great Wizard of Oz,' said Dorothy.

'Are you sure that Oz will see you?' asked the woman.

'Why wouldn't he?' said Dorothy.

'Because it's said he never lets anyone see him. I have been to the Emerald City many times. It's a beautiful and wonderful place, but I have never been permitted to see the Great Wizard. Nor do I know of anyone who has ever seen him!'

'Does he ever go out?' asked the Tin Man.

'Never,' replied the woman. 'He sits day after day in the great throne room of his palace.'

'What does he look like?' asked the Scarecrow.

'That is hard to tell,' said the woman. 'Oz is a great wizard and can take any form he chooses. Some say he looks like a bird. Some say he looks like an elephant. And some say he looks like a cat. To others he appears as an elf. Who the real Oz is, no living person can tell.'

'Oh, dear,' said Dorothy. 'We must at least try and see him or our journey will have been a waste of time!'

'Yes, I want him to give me some brains,' said the Scarecrow.

'Oh, Oz could do that easily,' said the woman. 'He has more brains than he needs.'

'And I want him to give me a heart,' said the Tin Man.

'That won't trouble him at all,' replied the woman. 'He has a large collection of hearts, of all shapes and sizes.'

'And does he have any courage to spare?' asked the Lion.

'Oz keeps a huge pot of courage beside him in the throne room,' she said. 'He'll be glad to give you some.'

'And can he send me back to Kansas?' asked Dorothy.

'Where is Kansas?' asked the woman. 'From here, I don't really know,' said Dorothy, 'but it's my home and I'm sure it's somewhere.'

'Oz can do anything,' answered the woman. 'I expect he'll be able to find Kansas for you. But first you must get to see him, and that will be a hard task.'

The next morning, they were up early and on the yellow brick road again. Almost immediately they noticed a green glow in the sky ahead of them.

'I wonder what that is?' said the Lion.

'Something very strange,' said the Tin Man.

The sky became greener and greener, the closer they got to the Emerald City.

It was late afternoon when they finally looked down from a low hill and saw the city itself.

No wonder there was a green glow in the sky. The whole place seemed to be built in green. The houses looked green. And the walls surrounding the city were built of green bricks.

Dorothy and her friends walked down to the city gates. They were studded with thousands

of brilliant green emeralds, glittering in the sinking sun.

There was a button beside the gate. Dorothy pushed it. She heard a bell ring inside. The big gates swung slowly open and they entered. Before them stood a little man, dressed in green from head to foot.

'What do you want in the Emerald City?' he asked.

'We've come to see the Great Wizard of Oz,' replied Dorothy.

The man was very surprised at her answer. 'It's been so many years since anyone asked to see Oz,' he said, shaking his head. 'I can't remember anyone ever seeing him. He is a powerful wizard. And if you have come for a foolish reason, he might be angry and destroy you all in an instant.'

'Ours is not a foolish reason!' exclaimed the Scarecrow. 'We're here on an important mission and we have been told that Oz is a good wizard!'

'So he is,' said the man, 'and he rules the Emerald City wisely and well. But few have ever dared to ask to see his face. I am the Guardian of the Gates and I have never seen it.'

He scratched his head for a moment and then agreed to escort them to the Palace of Oz.

Chapter 11

The Palace of Oz

Dorothy, Toto, the Scarecrow, the Tin Man and the Lion followed the Guardian of the Gates into the streets of the Emerald City.

They were dazzled by the wonderful sights. All the houses were built of green marble and studded with shining emeralds. The windows in the houses had green glass.

There were lots of people walking about. They were all dressed in green. The goods in the green shops were green. Even the chickens and their eggs were green!

It didn't take long to reach Oz's palace. There was a soldier with green whiskers and a green uniform at the palace gate.

'Here are some strangers who wish to see the Great Oz,' said the Guardian of the Gates.

'He never sees anyone,' said the soldier, 'but I'll tell Oz, the Great and the Terrible, that you have asked to see him.'

He went off and returned a few minutes later.

'Have you seen Oz?' asked Dorothy.

'Oh, no,' answered the soldier. 'I've never seen him. But I spoke with him as he sat behind a screen. He says he will see you. He didn't want to at first, but I told him about the red shoes you were wearing and the mark on your forehead. He seemed very interested in seeing you after that.'

The soldier said that Oz would only see them one at a time, and no more than one a day.

'So you will have to stay in the palace for a few days until he has seen you all,' he explained.

He took Dorothy and her friends into the castle and showed them their rooms.

Dorothy and Toto were given a beautiful room with a tiny fountain in the middle. There was a huge bed in a corner.

'Make yourself at home,' said the soldier, 'and if you wish for anything at all, just ring the bell on the wall.'

As for the others, the Scarecrow had the biggest room of all. But as he had no brain, he just stood in the doorway all night.

The Tin Man spent the night moving his arms and legs up and down in bed, to make sure they didn't rust up again.

The Lion would have preferred a pile of leaves in the forest to sleep on, but he too was given a huge bed. He curled himself up and went straight to sleep.

The next morning a maid came and fetched Dorothy and Toto. She dressed Dorothy in a fabulous dress of green satin and put a green silk ribbon around Toto's neck.

The maid led them to a large hall outside the throne room. It was packed with ladies and gentlemen of Oz's court.

'Are you really going to look on the face of Oz, the Great and Terrible?' whispered one of them, with an astonished look.

'Of course,' replied Dorothy.

Just then, a bell rang. 'You can go in now,' said the soldier, pointing to a small door.

Dorothy had never been so nervous. She wondered who she would meet on the other side of the door.

Chapter 12

The Wizard of Oz

Dorothy opened the door and entered the huge throne room.

The walls, ceiling and floor were covered with thousands of glittering emeralds. At the end of the room was a gigantic throne. And sitting on it was an enormous head.

The head had no body at all. There was no hair on it either, but it did have eyes, a nose and a mouth.

As Dorothy gazed at this amazing creature, the eyes suddenly turned and looked at her. Then the mouth moved.

'I am Oz, the Great and Terrible. Who are you? Why did you want to see me?'

The voice was not as loud or frightening as she thought it might be. So she took courage and replied. 'I am Dorothy, the very small and very meek. I have come for your help.'

The eyes looked at her for a moment. Then the voice spoke again. 'Where did you get the red shoes?'

Dorothy explained how they had once belonged to the Wicked Witch of the East. 'I was given them after my house fell on her and killed her,' she said.

'And where did the mark on your forehead come from?'

'That is where the Witch of the North kissed me when she told me I should come to you for help.'

'What can I do for you?' asked Oz.

'I want to get back to Kansas,' said Dorothy. 'That's where I live with my Aunt Em and Uncle Henry. They will be terribly worried about me being away so long. But I don't know the way back.'

'Why should I help you?' asked Oz.

'Because you are strong and I am weak,' said Dorothy. 'Because you are a great wizard.'

'You were strong enough to kill the Wicked Witch of the East,' said Oz.

'That just happened by accident,' explained Dorothy.

'Well,' said the Wizard, 'I can send you back to Kansas, but you must do something for me first. You must kill the Wicked Witch of the West.'

'But I can't!' exclaimed Dorothy.

'You killed the Wicked Witch of the East,' said Oz, 'and you have the shoes which bear a powerful charm. So surely you can rid the world of the other wicked witch. I give you my word. I will send you back to Kansas. But only when

I know that the Wicked Witch of the West is dead!'

Dorothy burst into tears. 'But I have never killed anyone or anything on purpose in my life. Even if I wanted to kill her, how could I do it?'

The face of Oz stared at her. 'That is my last word on the matter. Now remember this; the Witch of the West is wicked – really wicked. She deserves to be killed. Be gone and don't let me see you until the witch is dead!'

That night, Dorothy told her friends what had happened. They were very sorry for her.

The next morning the soldier with the green whiskers called for the Scarecrow. 'Oz wants to see you,' he said.

When the Scarecrow entered the throne room, he was surprised to see a beautiful lady, wearing the most wonderful silk dress, sitting on the throne.

'I am Oz, the Great and Terrible,' said the lady. 'Who are you and why do you want to see me?'

'I'm a scarecrow stuffed with straw. I've come to ask if you can give me some brains.'

'I will do what you ask,' said the voice of Oz. 'But only when you have done me a favour in return. I want you to kill the Wicked Witch of the West.'

'I thought you asked Dorothy to kill the witch,' said the Scarecrow.

'So I did,' said Oz. 'But I don't care who kills her. So don't come back until the witch is dead.'

It was the Tin Man's turn next. When he went in he saw neither a head nor a lady sitting on the throne. This time it was a terrible beast, as big as an elephant.

The beast had a head like a rhinoceros, but it had five eyes, five arms and five legs.

The voice of Oz asked the Tin Man what he wanted. Oz said he could easily find him a heart, but only after the Wicked Witch of the West was dead.

'When she's dead,' said Oz, 'I will give you the kindest and most loving heart you can imagine.'

The next day it was the Lion's turn.

The Lion entered the throne room and was astonished to see a ball of fire on the throne.

'What do you want of me?' asked the voice of Oz, from inside the ball of fire.

The Lion explained that he wanted courage.

'You shall have it,' said the voice, 'but only when you bring me proof that the Wicked Witch of the West is dead. Until then you will remain a coward.'

That night, Dorothy, Toto, the Scarecrow, the Tin Man and the Lion talked together about what they should do.

No one wanted to kill the witch, but they decided to go and find her anyway.

Chapter 13

The Search for the Wicked Witch

The next day, Dorothy and her friends left Oz's palace. Before they left the Emerald City, they asked the soldier with the green whiskers to show them the road that led to the Castle of the Wicked Witch of the West.

'There is no road,' said the soldier, 'because no one ever wants to go there. Everyone is too frightened of her.'

'Then how will we find the witch?'
asked Dorothy.

'The sun sets in the west,' he answered. 'That
is your direction. When you get there, you won't
need to find her. She will find you. But beware,
she is a wicked and fierce witch. Her people
are called the Winkies and they are sworn to
kill all her enemies. And if they don't get you,
her wicked wolves, cruel crows and stinging
bees will.'

Soon after, Dorothy and her friends left the
city, travelling towards the west. They were not
to know that the Wicked Witch of the West had
already seen them.

The witch only had one eye, but it was more
powerful than a telescope. She was sitting at
her castle gate when she saw Dorothy and her
friends cross the border into her country.

The Wicked Witch of the West was furious.
They had dared to enter her country without
permission!

She stamped up and down in anger and blew
on a silver whistle that hung around her neck.

Instantly, a pack of wolves with fierce eyes and sharp teeth ran to her.

She pointed to Dorothy and her friends. 'Tear them to pieces,' she cried. 'Tear them into tiny little pieces.'

The wolves dashed away towards the invaders.

It was lucky that the Tin Man and the Scarecrow saw the wolves coming.

'This is my fight!' cried the Tin Man. 'Get behind me!'

He seized his axe and was ready for them.

As the leader of the wolves reached him, Tin Man swung out with his axe. He killed the beast with one slash. His axe was already raised again by the time the second wolf arrived. It died instantly too.

Forty wolves attacked and forty wolves the Tin Man killed. At last they all lay in a great heap in front of him.

The Wicked Witch saw it all happen. She was angrier than ever. She blew her whistle twice.

This time the sky darkened, as a huge flock of crows suddenly appeared.

'King Crow!' screamed the Witch. 'Fly at the strangers! Peck out their eyes! Peck them to little pieces!'

The Scarecrow saw them coming. 'This is my battle!' he cried.

There's only one thing that crows are scared of, and that is a scarecrow. As soon as they saw the Scarecrow, most of them flew off. Only the King Crow and his guards were brave enough to stay.

'It is only a stuffed man,' screamed King Crow. 'I will peck his eyes out.'

The King Crow dived to attack. But the Scarecrow caught him by the neck and killed him.

A few other crows followed their leader. Each one met the same fate. The Scarecrow killed forty crows that day.

The Wicked Witch of the West saw it all. She went red in the face with fury and blew her whistle three times.

A gigantic swarm of bees appeared.

'Sting the strangers to death!' screamed the Witch. 'Sting them a hundred times.'

The Tin Man had another plan this time. He told the others to borrow some of the Scarecrow's stuffing and hide themselves beneath it. By the time the bees attacked, the Scarecrow was just a pile of empty clothes. They had emptied him of stuffing.

When the bees arrived, all they could see was the Tin Man. They attacked him in their thousands. Each one broke their stinger on his metal body. They flew off home, buzzing in pain.

Afterwards, Dorothy and the Lion put the straw back in the Scarecrow. He was as good as new again.

The Wicked Witch now sent her slaves, the Winkies, to attack. They were armed with sharp spears.

The Winkies were not brave people and only did what the Witch ordered because they had to. As soon as the Lion roared, they ran away.

The Witch knew she had one more weapon.

She went and found her Golden Cap.

This cap had a charm attached to it. Whoever owned it could call upon the Winged Monkeys for help. But no person could command these creatures more than three times.

The Wicked Witch had used the charmed cap twice already. The first time the Winged Monkeys had made the Winkies her slaves. And the second time they had brought her the wolves, crows and bees.

With her wolves, crows and bees gone, the Witch decided to use up her last wish.

She put the golden cap on her head, placed her hat on top of it, stood on one leg and started a chant. 'Ep-ep-ep, kak-ke! Hil-lo, hol-lo hel-lo! Ziz-zy, zuz-zy, zik!'

Immediately the sky filled with hundreds of Winged Monkeys.

'Go to the strangers!' screamed the Witch. 'Destroy all of them except the Lion. I'll turn him into a horse and make him work for me!'

Dorothy and her friends saw the flying monkeys approach. This time no one knew what to do.

Chapter 14

Captured!

The Tin Man was the first to be captured. A Winged Monkey swooped out of the sky and caught him with its powerful hands. The monkey flew off, circling higher and higher into the sky. Then it dropped the Tin Man onto the large rocks below. The Tin Man was so battered and dented he could not move.

Next, a group of flying monkeys caught the Scarecrow and pulled out all the straw from his head, arms and body. Then they bundled up his hat, boots and clothes and threw them into a tall tree.

Other monkeys tied up the Lion with coils of rope and flew away with him to the Witch's castle.

The largest of all the Winged Monkeys swooped down on Dorothy. The creature was about to attack when it saw the mark on her forehead that had been left by the Good Witch's kiss.

The monkey landed close by and warned the others not to attack Dorothy. 'We must not harm this little girl,' he said. 'She is protected by the Power of Good from the Good Witch's kiss. And that is greater than the Power of Evil. All we can do is carry her and her dog safely to the castle.'

And that is what they did.

When the Wicked Witch of the West saw Dorothy, she asked her what she knew about the mark on her forehead and the red shoes. 'Why, nothing,' Dorothy replied. 'The Good Witch of the North kissed me on the forehead and she also gave me the shoes. She said they were charmed but didn't know how.'

A horrible smile crossed the Wicked Witch's face. She was glad that Dorothy did not understand the powers she had been given.

'You will be my slave for the rest of your life,' said the Witch. 'From now on, you will do everything I say.'

The Witch ordered Dorothy into the castle kitchen and made her clean all the pots and sweep the floor.

Then she went to change the Lion into a horse. But the Lion roared so loudly when he saw her that even the Witch was frightened.

'If you come any closer,' said the Lion, 'I will eat you!'

'Then I shall starve you until you are too weak to bite me,' replied the Witch, before leaving him alone.

That night Dorothy found her way from the kitchen to the courtyard, where the Lion was kept. She brought him some food and as he ate, they planned how to escape the Witch's clutches.

Dorothy was beginning to think she would never see her Aunty Em or Uncle Henry again.

But if Dorothy was not very happy, neither was the Witch.

The Wicked Witch of the West had lost her wolves, crows and bees. She had also used up her last request for help from the Winged Monkeys. Yet, she knew that if she could steal Dorothy's red shoes they would give her more power than ever. The trouble was that the magic red shoes were more powerful than her own magic. Her only chance to steal them would be if Dorothy took them off.

But Dorothy found them so comfortable that she never took them off.

The Witch tried everything. She asked Dorothy to lend them to her so she could clean them for her. She offered to free Dorothy and her friends in exchange for the shoes. But Dorothy would not part with the shoes.

The Witch was furious. So she tried one last trick. She placed an invisible iron bar across the floor in the courtyard. She then called on

The house filled with wind and Dorothy felt it lift off the ground and whirl up into the sky!

'The road to the Emerald City,' the Witch of the North said,
'is paved with yellow brick. So you cannot miss it.'

'Do you think,' asked the Scarecrow, 'that if I went to the
Emerald City, the Wizard could give me some brains?'

Dorothy oiled the Tin Man's joints until he could move *again*.

A great lion leaped out onto the road ahead of them
and let out a ferocious roar!

Dorothy and Toto ran into the field of brilliant
red flowers and were soon fast asleep.

They reached a huge city that seemed to be built in green. It was studded
with thousands of brilliant green emeralds, glittering in the sun.

Dorothy picked up a bucket of water and
splashed its contents over the witch.

'I'm just an ordinary little man,' said Oz.

Glinda offered to help Dorothy get home to Kansas.

'My darling child!' cried Aunt Em, hugging and kissing Dorothy.
'Where in the world have you come from?'

Dorothy, who immediately tripped over the bar, causing one of her shoes to fall off.

The Wicked Witch swooped down and gathered it up instantly. Now she owned half the power of the shoes!

'Give me back my shoe!' shouted Dorothy.

'I won't!' shrieked the Witch. 'And some day I will get the other one too!'

Dorothy was furious. She looked around for something to attack the Witch with. There was nothing but a bucket of water.

Dorothy picked it up. The Witch's face suddenly went white with terror.

'Don't do it!' she screamed.

It was too late. Dorothy threw the bucket at the Witch.

The Witch let out a terrible scream. 'See what you've done. I'm melting away!'

Dorothy was shocked to see the Witch was indeed starting to melt away before her very eyes.

'Didn't you know that water would be the end of me?' asked the vanishing Witch, in a wailing, terrified voice.

'Of course not,' replied Dorothy. 'How should I know that?'

'Well,' said the Witch, 'in a few minutes I will be gone. I have been a wicked witch indeed, but I never thought a little girl like you would end my days. Look out! Here I go!'

With those words, the Witch fell down and her last remains turned into a brown, shapeless mess.

The only thing that was left of the Witch was the single red shoe. Dorothy picked it up and put it back on her foot.

Chapter 15

Free Again

Dorothy ran to tell the Lion that he was free again. She also went and spoke to the Winkies to tell them that they were no longer slaves.

'If only the Scarecrow and the Tin Man were with us, then I would be truly happy,' said the Lion.

'We must go and find them,' said Dorothy, 'and we'll take the Winkies with us to help.'

When they finally found the Tin Man, he

was all battered and in bits and pieces. His axe lay beside him, but the blade was rusted and the handle broken off.

The Winkies lifted him up and carried him back to the Castle. Dorothy cried all the way. She felt so sorry for her friend.

When they got to the Castle, Dorothy asked the Winkies if any of them could mend the Tin Man.

'We are experts in working with tin,' said their leader. 'We can easily mend him.'

So they set to work. They worked for four days and nights, hammering, twisting and bending the Tin Man back into shape. They even sharpened the axe and put a new handle on it.

The Winkies did a wonderful job. He might have had a few tin patches put here and there to hide the odd hole but the Tin Man was almost as good as new.

When he walked into Dorothy's room, she burst into tears of happiness. The Tin Man might have cried too, but Dorothy warned him not to. She didn't want his joints to rust up again.

As for the Lion, he was so happy that he cried too. He wiped the tears from his eyes with the end of his tail.

Now that the Tin Man was mended, Dorothy's thoughts turned to the Scarecrow.

Once more, she called on the Winkies to help. They searched the country for days until, eventually, the Lion spotted his clothes in the tree where the Winged Monkeys had thrown them.

The Winkies collected all the clothes and took them back to the Castle.

Dorothy stuffed them all with nice, clean straw. It was as if a miracle had happened, for the Scarecrow was as good as before. He was so happy to be alive again.

So Dorothy and all her friends were together again. And now that the Wicked Witch was dead, it was time to return to the Emerald City.

'We must go back to Oz,' said Dorothy, 'because we have done what he asked us to do. Now he must keep his promises to us.'

'Yes,' said the Tin Man, 'at last I shall get my heart.'

'And I'll get my brains,' added the Scarecrow.

'I'll get my courage,' said the Lion.

'And I'll get back to Kansas!' cried Dorothy.

The Winkies were sorry to hear they were going. They had grown especially fond of Tin Man. They wanted him to stay behind and rule over them, as King.

Before they left, Dorothy went to the Wicked Witch's cupboard to get some food for the journey. There she found the Witch's Golden Cap.

Dorothy did not know about the power of the cap. She just thought how pretty it was. She put it on her head and found it fitted perfectly.

It was now late at night, but no one wanted to stay another minute in the Witch's castle.

So rather than wait for morning, they set off for the Emerald City in the dark.

Chapter 16

The Golden Cap

As there was no road between the castle of the Wicked Witch and the Emerald City, Dorothy and her friends were soon lost. They walked all night and by the next morning, they did not know where they were.

'If we walk far enough,' said Dorothy, 'we'll surely find some place or other.'

But day after day they travelled and found nothing.

'I'll never get any brains now,' said the Scarecrow.

'Nor I my heart,' added the Tin Man.

'And I don't think I have the courage to keep on walking much further,' said the Lion. Finally, Dorothy lost heart too. She sat down on the grass and looked at her companions. Toto was exhausted.

Suddenly, she had an idea. 'Why don't we call the field mice!' she cried. 'They told us to call if ever we needed them. All we have to do is shout as loud as we can, and they'll hear us. That's what their Queen said.'

'Why didn't we think of that before!' exclaimed the Scarecrow.

So they all shouted out, calling for the field mice.

In moments, Dorothy and her friends were surrounded by hundreds of the mice. They arrived with their Queen.

'What can we do for you?' she asked.

'We've lost our way,' explained Dorothy.

'Which is the way to the Emerald City?'

'Oh,' she said. 'You must have been walking in the opposite direction. You are far, far away.' Just then, the Queen noticed Dorothy's Golden Cap.

'Why don't you use the charm of your cap,' she said, 'and call up the Winged Monkeys. They'll carry you to the city in minutes.'

'I didn't know the cap had a charm,' said Dorothy. 'What is it?'

'You can use the cap three times to ask for help from the Winged Monkeys,' explained the Queen of the Field Mice. 'The instructions are written inside the cap.'

Dorothy looked and saws the magic words. She began chanting. 'Ep-ep-ep, kak-ke! Hil-lo, hol-lo hel-lo! Ziz-zy, zuz-zy, zik!'

The Lion, the Scarecrow and the Tin Man were very puzzled. No one had told them anything about the Golden Cap.

Suddenly, there was the sound of flapping wings as several Winged Monkeys flew down.

'What is your command?' asked the King of the Winged Monkeys.

'We wish to go to Emerald City,' said Dorothy.

'We will carry you there,' replied the King. No sooner had he spoken than the King and another Winged Monkey caught Dorothy in their arms, and flew away with her.

Other monkeys picked up Toto, the Scarecrow, the Lion and the Tin Man.

At first, the Scarecrow and the Tin Man were frightened. They remembered how badly the Winged Monkeys had treated them before. But they stopped worrying as soon as they saw the monkeys meant them no harm now.

On the way, Dorothy asked the King of the Winged Monkeys why they obeyed the charms of the Golden Cap.

It was a long story, he said. But Dorothy wanted to hear it. So as they flew towards Emerald City, the King told her the story.

Chapter 17

Mischievous Monkeys

'Once upon a time,' said the King of the Winged Monkeys, 'we were free, living happily in the great forest. But, perhaps some of us were rather too full of mischief at times.

'We often flew down and pulled the tails of the animals that had no wings. We chased the birds and threw nuts at people walking in the forest. This all happened long before Oz came out of the clouds to rule this land.

'Now, at this time there was a princess called Giselle who was also a powerful sorceress. She lived in a huge palace and used all her magic for good things. She never hurt anyone.

'Then she fell in love with a boy called Kela. Giselle loved him dearly and looked forward to their wedding day.

'On the morning of their wedding, we spotted him walking by the river. He was dressed in his wedding costume; a rich costume of pink silk and yellow velvet.

'One of our naughtiest monkeys swooped down and lifted him into the air, and dropped him into the river. Kela swam to shore, but his fine clothes were ruined.

'The Princess was very angry. And for the first time in her life, she cast a bad spell on all of us.

'She gave her husband the Golden Cap as a wedding present. It wasn't an ordinary Golden Cap – whoever owned it was given the power of three wishes. And our punishment was to spend the rest of our lives carrying out those wishes. We were to be the slaves of the Golden Cap and its owner forever.

'Kela used his three wishes to make us carry him on three long journeys. Then he gave the Golden Cap to the Wicked Witch of the West.

'Her first wish was to use us to capture the Winkies and make them her slaves. For her second wish, we gave her an army of wolves, crows and bees. The third, and last wish, was for us to capture you and your friends.'

'But now the Golden Cap is yours. So you have the right to ask three wishes.'

As the King finished his story, Dorothy looked down and saw the green, shining walls of the Emerald City below.

The Winged Monkeys set the travellers down by the entrance to the Palace of Oz. The soldier with the green whiskers was still on guard.

'What! Are you back again?' he asked. 'I thought you had gone to find the Wicked Witch of the West.'

'We did find her,' said the Scarecrow, 'and she was melted into nothing.'

'Melted!' cried the soldier. 'Well, that is good news, indeed. Who melted her?'

'It was Dorothy,' said the Lion.

'Good gracious!' he exclaimed, bowing to Dorothy for doing such a splendid deed.

Then he let them inside the castle.

A maid showed them to their old rooms, while the soldier went to give Oz the news. Dorothy and her friends expected to be called in immediately, to see the wizard. But they heard nothing.

For three days they were kept waiting. Eventually, they asked the soldier to tell Oz again that they were waiting to see him. Finally, they got their answer. Oz would see them at nine o'clock the next morning.

That night, Dorothy dreamed of being back in Kansas. The Scarecrow dreamed of getting a brain. The Tin Man dreamed of having a heart. And the Lion dreamed of waking up full of courage.

In the morning, the green-whiskered soldier escorted them to see Oz.

Chapter 18

The Secret of Oz

Dorothy, Toto, the Scarecrow, the Tin Man and the Lion entered the green throne room. Each one of them expected to see Oz in the shape they had seen him in before.

They were all very surprised to see no one in the room at all.

Suddenly, a voice boomed out. 'I am Oz, the Great and Terrible. Why have you come back to see me?'

The voice terrified them. But Dorothy was brave enough to ask where Oz was.

'I am everywhere,' the voice replied, 'and today I am invisible. I shall now go and sit on my throne, so you can talk to me.'

Still they saw no one. So Dorothy walked up and spoke to the empty throne. 'We have come to claim our promise, oh Great and Terrible one.'

'What promise?' asked Oz's voice, from the throne.

'You promised to send me back to Kansas when the Wicked Witch of the West was destroyed.'

'And you promised to give me brains,' added the Scarecrow.

'Courage was my reward,' said the Lion.

'A heart was mine,' said the Tin Man.

'Is the Wicked Witch really destroyed?' asked the voice.

'Yes. I melted her to nothing with a bucket of water,' said Dorothy.

'Dear me!' said the voice. 'What a sudden way for her to go. Well, come back tomorrow. I need time to think about what you have told me.'

This made them all angry.

'You've had plenty of time to think!' cried the Tin Man.

'We won't wait a day longer,' added the Scarecrow.

'You must keep your promise,' said Dorothy. The Lion decided to try and frighten Oz. He gave such a large roar that Toto jumped in the air and landed on a screen that stood behind the throne. Seeing something behind it, Toto pulled the screen back further.

What Dorothy and her friends saw next filled them with wonder.

Standing behind the screen was a little old man with a wrinkled face, wearing a large pair of spectacles and a top hat. He seemed to be as surprised as they were.

The Tin Man was still angry and he raised his axe, and ran towards the little man. 'Who are you?' he shouted.

'I am Oz, the Great and Terrible,' said the man, in a trembling voice. 'Please don't hit me. I'll do anything you want me to.'

They all looked at the little man with surprise and dismay.

'I thought Oz was a great head,' said Dorothy.

'To me, Oz was a beautiful lady,' said the Scarecrow.

'I thought Oz was a terrible beast,' said the Tin Man.

'I thought he was a ball of fire,' said the Lion.

The little man continued to tremble. 'You are all correct,' he said, meekly. 'I have been playing make-believe.'

'What!' cried Dorothy. 'Aren't you a great wizard?'

'Hush my dear, my people might hear you,' replied the little man. 'Then I will be ruined. I am supposed to be a great wizard.'

'And aren't you?' asked Dorothy.

'Not a bit of it, my dear. I'm just an ordinary little man.'

'You're more than that,' said the Scarecrow angrily. 'You're a humbug and a cheat.'

'Exactly,' agreed the man, rubbing his hands together as though he was proud of the fact. 'I am a humbug and a cheat.'

'But this is terrible,' replied the Tin Man. 'How will I get a heart? How will the Lion get his courage? How will the Scarecrow get a brain? And how will Dorothy get back to Kansas?'

'My dear friends,' said Oz, 'I'd rather you didn't mention those things. Just think of the trouble I would be in if all the people knew I was a fraud.'

'Does anyone else know your secret, apart from us?' asked the Lion.

'No,' said Oz. 'I have fooled everyone for so long, I thought I would never be found out.'

'How did you appear to me as a head?' asked Dorothy.

Oz took Dorothy and her friends to a small room behind the throne. Leaning on the wall was a huge face made out of cardboard.

'I just hung it from the ceiling above the throne, and made the eyes and mouth move with string.'

'What about the voice?' she inquired.

'I am a ventriloquist. I can throw the sound of my voice wherever I want to.'

Oz showed them the dress and mask he wore to play the part of the beautiful lady, and the costume he'd worn as the beast. The ball of fire was just a big ball of cotton he'd hung up and set fire to.

'You should be ashamed of yourself!' cried the Lion.

'Oh, I am. I certainly am,' replied the little man. 'But there was nothing else I could do. If you would like, I will tell you my story.'

So they all patiently waited for Oz to begin.

Chapter 19

Oz's Story

'I was born in Omaha, not far from Kansas,' began Oz. 'When I grew up, I became a ventriloquist. I could imitate any bird or beast.

'I soon became tired of that, so I became a balloonist. I used to go up in a balloon on circus days, to attract the crowds. But one day I went up and couldn't come down again.

'The balloon went up into the clouds, so high that it was caught by a great wind. For a day and a night I travelled across the skies. On the morning of the second day I awoke to find myself over a strange and beautiful country.

'When the balloon finally returned to the ground, I landed in the middle of a huge crowd of people. I was so frightened that I hid from them, under the balloon. I eventually spoke to them, but I still didn't let them see me. They all thought I must be a great wizard because I had appeared from the clouds.

'Of course, I let them think that because they were afraid of me. They promised to do anything I asked of them.

'I was a young man then, so just to amuse myself, I asked them to build this city. The whole land was covered in emeralds so I told them to cover the buildings with jewels.

'I am very old now, but I still think the Emerald City is a beautiful place. I have been good to the people and they like me, but ever since this palace was built, I have shut myself up so no one could see who I really was.

'My great terror was the Witches. I had no

magical powers, but I soon found out that they did. There were four of them in this country. They ruled the people in the North, South, East and West. Fortunately, the Witches of the North and South were good, and I knew they would do me no harm.

'The Witches of the East and West were terribly wicked, but they imagined I was more powerful than them. That's why they didn't come to destroy me.

'I lived in terror of those two witches finding out the truth. So you can imagine how pleased I was when I heard that your house had fallen on

the Wicked Witch of the East.

'Now you have killed the Wicked Witch of the West too. But I have no real powers and so I am truly ashamed that I cannot keep my promises.'

Dorothy looked at Oz for a moment. Then she spoke. 'I think you are a very bad man.'

'Oh, no, my dear,' Oz replied. 'I'm really a very good man, but I will admit to being a very bad wizard.'

'Can't you give me brains?' asked the Scarecrow.

'You don't need them,' said Oz. 'You are learning new things every day. A baby has brains but it doesn't know much when it is born. The longer you live, the more you know.'

'That may be true,' said the Scarecrow, 'but I shall never be happy unless you give me brains.'

The false wizard looked at him carefully. 'Well,' he said, with a sigh. 'I'm not a good magician, but if you come to me tomorrow morning, maybe I can fill your head with brains.

But I will not be able to tell you how to use them. You must find that out for yourself.'

'Oh, thank you! Thank you!' cried the Scarecrow. 'I will find a way to use them, never fear!'

'And how about my courage?' asked the Lion.

'I'm sure you already have plenty of courage,' replied the little man. 'All you need is confidence in yourself. There is no living thing that is not afraid when it faces danger. True courage is in facing danger when you are afraid. And you have lots of that kind of courage.'

'But I won't be truly happy,' said the Lion, 'unless you give me courage.'

'Very well,' said the little man. 'Come and see me tomorrow morning. I'll see what I can do.'

'How about my heart?' asked the Tin Man.

'I think you are wrong to want a heart,' said Oz. 'A heart can make you unhappy. If only you knew it, you are lucky not to have a heart.'

'That's a matter of opinion,' said the Tin Man. 'But I shall be happy to bear that unhappiness if you give me a heart.'

'Oh, well then,' said Oz. 'Come to me tomorrow and I'll try and find you a heart. I have played being a wizard for so many years, I may as well continue a little longer.'

Dorothy was the last to speak. 'And how am I to get back to Kansas?'

Oz said he would have to think about that. 'I shall need a few days. I'll try to find a way to carry you over the desert. In the meantime, you will stay in the palace as my guests. There is one thing, though. I beg of you that you keep my secret from my people.'

They agreed not to say anything about what they had learned and went back to their rooms in the palace.

Dorothy cried herself to sleep that night. She saw no way of ever getting back to Kansas now.

As for Oz, he was desperately trying to think how he could make everyone's wishes come true.

Late that night, he had a brilliant idea.

Chapter 20

Oz's Magic

The next morning, the Scarecrow was very excited.

'I'm going to Oz to get my brains today,' he cried. 'When I come back I shall be as clever as everyone else.'

'I always liked you as you were,' said Dorothy.

'It's kind of you to like a scarecrow,' said the Scarecrow, 'but surely you'll think even more of me when you hear the great thoughts my new brain will come up with.'

'We'll see about that,' she answered. Then he was off to see Oz.

'I have come for my brains,' said the Scarecrow, a little nervously.

'Oh, yes,' said Oz. 'Now sit down in the chair, please. You must excuse me for taking your head off first, but I shall have to do it, in order to put your brains in their proper place.'

'That's all right,' said the Scarecrow. 'You are quite welcome to take my head off, as long as it will be a better one when you put it back.'

So the Wizard of Oz took off the Scarecrow's head and emptied out the straw. Then he went into the little room behind the throne.

If the Scarecrow could have seen what Oz did next, he would have been very surprised.

Oz pulled out a bag of bran – a kind of cereal food. He mixed the bran with a bag of pins and needles, and poured the mixture into the Scarecrow's head. Then he stuffed the rest of the head with straw.

He returned to the Scarecrow and fastened his head on again. 'From now on,' said Oz, 'you will be a wise man. I have given you *brand* new brains.'

The Scarecrow was delighted, and hurried back to join his friends. He had no idea that Oz had filled his head with bran, rather than brand new brains, but it made no difference to the Scarecrow. He thought he had been given a proper brain, so he acted as if he had one.

Dorothy looked at him curiously. There were pins and needles bulging out of the top of his head.

'How do you feel?' she asked.

'Oh, very wise indeed,' he replied. 'I shall know everything by the time I get used to my new brains.'

'Why are those needles and pins sticking out of your head?' she asked.

The Lion came up with an answer. 'That is the proof that he is now very sharp-witted.'

The Tin Man smiled and went off to see Oz.

'I have come for my heart,' he said.

'Very good,' said Oz, 'but I shall have to cut a hole in your chest, so I can put the heart in the right place. I hope it doesn't hurt.'

'Oh, no,' answered the Tin Man. 'I won't feel it at all.'

Oz brought a pair of powerful scissors and cut a small hole in the Tin Man's chest. Then he went to the room behind his throne and collected a very pretty heart. It was made of silk and stuffed with sawdust.

'Isn't it a beauty!' he exclaimed.

'It is indeed,' replied the Tin Man, who was very pleased. 'But is it a kind heart? I wouldn't want a cruel one.'

'Oh, it's a very kind heart,' said Oz, putting it in the Tin Man's chest. Then he patched up the hole with another bit of tin, on which he had drawn a love heart.

'I am very grateful to you and shall never forget your kindness,' said the Tin Man.

It was the Lion's turn next.

'I've come for my courage,' he said to Oz.

'Oh, yes,' replied Oz. 'I'll go and get it for you.'

Once more Oz went into his special room and took down a green bottle from a shelf. He returned to the Lion and told him to take a drink from the bottle. 'What is in it?' asked the Lion.

'Well,' replied Oz, 'once inside you, the liquid turns into courage. Courage is always inside people. So I advise you to drink it as soon as possible.'

The Lion did not hesitate. He emptied the bottle in one huge swallow.

'How do you feel now?' asked Oz.

'Full of courage!' roared the Lion.

So the Lion returned to his friends, happier than ever. He wasn't to know that the only contents inside the bottle were water. But it was enough to make him believe he was full of courage.

Meanwhile in the throne room, Oz smiled to himself. He was delighted that he had managed to give the Scarecrow, the Tin Man and the Lion exactly what they thought they wanted.

'How can I help being a humbug and a fraud,' he laughed. 'I only did what Dorothy's friends wanted. All they needed was to believe that I could do something . . . even if I couldn't.'

Then the Wizard of Oz started thinking again. 'It will take more imagination to carry Dorothy back to Kansas,' he said, scratching his head. 'I'm sure I don't know how it can be done.'

Chapter 21

A Plan for Dorothy

Dorothy heard nothing from Oz for three days. She was beginning to lose hope. But her friends were so happy.

The Scarecrow told her how his head was full of new ideas. He said he couldn't tell her what they were, because only he was clever enough to understand them.

The Tin Man said he had never known a kinder or more loving heart.

And the Lion declared he was now afraid of nothing on earth.

On the fourth day, Oz finally sent for Dorothy.

'Sit down, my dear,' he said. 'I think I have found a way to get you out of this country.'

'And back to Kansas?' she asked eagerly. 'Well, I'm not sure about Kansas,' said Oz, 'because I haven't the faintest idea in which direction it lies. But the first thing you must do is cross the desert. After that it will be easier to find your way home.'

'How can I cross the desert?' asked Dorothy.

'I'll tell you how I think you can do it,' he replied. 'When I first came to this country, I arrived by balloon. You also came by air. You were carried by a huge wind. So I am convinced the best way to get across the desert will be through the air.'

Oz said it was impossible for him to make a big wind, but he thought he could build another balloon.

'How?' asked Dorothy.

Oz explained that a balloon was only made of silk and filled with gas, or hot air. 'I've got plenty of silk in the palace,' he said, 'but there's no gas. We'll have to make do with hot air.'

Oz warned Dorothy that hot air wasn't as good as gas. It might grow cold and then the balloon would sink to the ground. 'Then we would be lost,' he said.

'You mean you're coming with me?' said Dorothy.

'Yes, of course,' replied Oz. 'I am tired of being a humbug and a fraud. One day my people will find out the truth. So I'd rather go back to Kansas with you. I could join the circus again.'

'I shall be glad to have your company,' said Dorothy.

'Then I shall begin,' he replied. 'I'll find the silk for the balloon first and you can help me sew it together.'

It took Oz and Dorothy three days to sew all the pieces of silk together. Then he sent the

soldier with the green whiskers to find a basket
to hang beneath the balloon.

When it was all ready, Oz announced to his
people that he was going to visit a great brother
wizard who lived in the clouds.

The news quickly spread and everyone came
to see him off.

Oz ordered his servants to carry the balloon
to the front of the palace. There the Tin Man
had chopped up a huge pile of wood. When the
firewood was lit, it sent clouds of hot air into the
balloon. When the balloon was full of hot air, it
would rise into the sky.

Oz and Dorothy climbed into the basket,
and the Tin Man added more wood to the fire.
'While I am gone,' Oz told his people, 'the
Scarecrow will rule in my place. You must obey
all his orders.'

Suddenly, Dorothy realised she had lost
Toto. She leapt out of the balloon and started
searching for him. At last she found him.
Together they hurried back to the balloon.

She was within a few steps of the balloon when the ropes holding it suddenly snapped. The balloon rose into the air without her.

'Come back!' she screamed. 'I must go with you!'

'I can't come back now,' Oz shouted, as the balloon climbed ever higher into the sky. 'Good-bye!'

And that was the last any of them ever saw of the Wonderful Wizard of Oz. He never came back, and he was never heard of again.

The people of Oz, however, remembered him with much love and affection. They never ever guessed he was a humbug and a fraud.

Besides, they all seemed happy to be ruled by a very wise and brainy Scarecrow.

Chapter 22

Trapped in the Land of Oz!

Dorothy cried for days after Oz vanished into the skies. She saw no hope at all of getting home to Kansas. She also missed the old rogue as much as the others.

'He gave me such a lovely heart,' said the Tin Man. 'I shall now cry a little in his memory, as long as Dorothy will wipe away my tears so I don't rust up.'

'With pleasure,' said Dorothy.

She dried each tear as it fell. When he had finished, he thanked her and oiled himself.

The Scarecrow was no wizard, but the people of the Emerald City were proud of him.

'We are the only city in the world,' they boasted, 'that is ruled by a stuffed man.'

One morning after Oz vanished into the skies, the four travellers were talking in the throne room at the palace. The Scarecrow, of course, was sitting on the throne.

'A short time ago I was up a pole in a farmer's field,' he said with a smile, 'and now I am the ruler of a beautiful city. I am quite happy with my lot.'

'I am too,' said the Tin Man. 'I only wanted a proper heart and now I have one.'

'As for me,' said the Lion, 'I am happy that I am now as brave a beast that ever lived, if not braver.'

'If only Dorothy was content to live here,' said the Scarecrow, 'we could all be happy together.'

'But I don't want to live here,' cried Dorothy.

'I want to go back to Kansas and live with Uncle Henry and Aunt Em.'

The Scarecrow started to think what could be done. He thought so hard that the pins and needles began to stick out of his brains.

'I know!' he said finally. 'Why not call the Winged Monkeys and ask them to carry you over the desert?'

'You clever Scarecrow!' cried Dorothy. 'I never thought of that. I'll go and get the Golden Cap.'

She returned with the charmed cap and said the magic words. The Winged Monkeys appeared immediately.

'This is the second time you have called us,' said the Monkey King. 'What do you wish?'

'I want you to fly me to Kansas,' said Dorothy.

'It cannot be done,' he replied sadly. 'We cannot leave this country. There has never been a Winged Monkey in Kansas and I don't suppose there ever will be. We will be glad to serve you in any other way, but we cannot cross the desert. Goodbye.'

Dorothy was so miserable. She had wasted her second wish. Now she could only call on the Winged Monkeys once more.

They decided to ask the soldier with the green whiskers for advice. So he was summoned into the presence of the new ruler of the Emerald City – the Scarecrow.

'Soldier with the green whiskers,' asked the Scarecrow, 'how can Dorothy cross the desert?'

'I cannot say,' he answered. 'I don't think anybody has ever crossed the desert except, perhaps, for Oz, the Great and Terrible. Maybe Glinda can help.'

'Who is Glinda?' inquired the Scarecrow.

'Glinda is the Witch of the South,' replied the soldier. 'She is the most powerful witch and rules over a people called the Quadlings. Her castle stands on the edge of the desert. So she may know a way across it.'

'How do I get to her castle?' asked Dorothy.

'Take the path to the south,' said the soldier. 'But be warned; there are wild beasts in the woods, and dangerous men live on that road. They don't like strangers crossing their land.'

Dorothy made up her mind immediately. 'I shall go and seek out the Witch of the South.'

'Then I shall come too,' said the Lion. 'I am really a wild beast, so I can protect you.'

'I shall go too,' said the Tin Man. 'My axe may help you.'

'When shall we start?' asked the Scarecrow. 'You might need my brains.'

'Are you coming too?' the others asked in surprise.

'Of course,' said Scarecrow. 'If it wasn't for Dorothy, I would never have got my brains. All my good luck is due to her. So I will never leave her until I know she is safely on her way home.'

Dorothy was so grateful that all her friends were coming with her.

'We'll leave tomorrow morning!' ordered His Majesty, the Great and Terrible Scarecrow, the Wise Ruler of Emerald City.

Chapter 23

Attacked by Trees

The next morning, the soldier with the green whiskers escorted Dorothy and her friends as far as the city gates.

'Remember,' he said to the Scarecrow, 'you must come back as soon as possible. You are our ruler and we cannot do without you.'

'I certainly shall,' the Scarecrow replied, 'but I must help Dorothy get home first.'

So they finally left the Emerald City.

'Oz was not such a bad wizard,' said the Tin Man, looking back to the Palace of Oz.

'He knew how to give me brains,' said the Scarecrow.

'And if Oz had given himself the courage he gave me, he would have been a brave man,' said the Lion.

'He was a bad wizard,' said Dorothy, 'but he wasn't a bad man.'

The Lion was particularly happy to be on the road to the south. 'City life does not agree with me,' he said. 'I want to show the other beasts in the wild how courageous I have become.'

Just then, the track entered a thick wood. The Scarecrow was in the lead. He had just walked beneath the first tree when its branches bent down and grabbed hold of him.

The Scarecrow was astonished. He had never heard of anyone being attacked by trees before. The branches lifted him high into the air, and then dropped him to the ground. He wasn't hurt, but he was mighty surprised.

The Scarecrow walked forward again. Once more he was grabbed by the branches and thrown into the air.

'This is most strange,' said Dorothy. 'What can we do?'

'The tree seems to have decided to stop our journey,' replied the Lion.

The Tin Man stepped forward. 'We shall see about this,' he said.

He walked beneath the tree. Immediately the branches reached out, ready to grab him. He quickly swung his axe and chopped the branch in two.

The tree shrieked, as if it was in pain. 'Come on!' shouted the Tin Man. 'Be quick!'

They all ran forward and safely passed under the tree. But a small branch caught Toto. The Tin Man quickly chopped it off and set the dog free.

The other trees in the forest did nothing to stop them, and they walked on.

Some hours later, they emerged from the forest to find the path blocked by a huge wall. 'Never mind,' said the Tin Man. 'I'll chop some wood and make a ladder to climb over it.'

It didn't take long, and the Tin Man was the first to climb up. 'How strange!' he exclaimed, when he looked over the top.

Dorothy was next to the top. 'Oh, how very strange!' she cried.

The Scarecrow and the Lion came next. They looked over and spoke as one. 'Oh, my! How very, very strange.'

Toto came last. He looked over the wall and barked.

Below them all was a great stretch of country. Scattered around were lots of tiny houses, all made from china.

The biggest of the houses were only as high as Dorothy's waist. There were tiny farms surrounded by walls of china. Even the cows, pigs, sheep and chickens were all made of china. Yet they mooed, snorted, baa-ed and clucked as if they were real.

There were people too; shepherds in pink trousers, milkmaids in blue, Princes and Princesses in splendid clothes, and lots of ordinary folk.

The tallest of these people did not reach as high as Dorothy's knee. 'How very, very strange indeed,' she thought.

Chapter 24

China Country

'How shall we get down from the wall?' asked Dorothy, who was determined that nothing should stop their journey.

The Scarecrow volunteered to jump down first. 'Then you can all jump onto me,' he said. He leapt down and one by one, the others followed, using him as a soft mattress to land on.

When they were all safely down, the Scarecrow was almost flat. The Lion kicked him here and there, and soon got his stuffing back into place.

They walked through the china village. The first person they came to was a china milkmaid, milking a cow. As they got near, the cow suddenly gave a kick.

The milkmaid tumbled over and so did the cow. Dorothy was shocked to see that the cow had broken its leg.

'There!' cried the milkmaid, looking fiercely at Dorothy. 'Look what you've done! You frightened the cow and it's broken its leg. I shall have to take it to be glued on again.'

'I'm sorry,' said Dorothy.

'So am I,' said the milkmaid. 'It's so hard being small and made of china.'

'But why are you small and made of china?' asked Dorothy.

'We upset the Wicked Witch of the East one day,' replied the little milkmaid. 'So she turned us all into tiny people made of china.'

Dorothy felt so sorry for the milkmaid and her people.

A little further on, Dorothy met a beautiful Princess.

'Oh, do be careful with me,' said the Princess. 'Don't break me.'

'But you could be mended, couldn't you?' replied Dorothy.

'Yes, I could,' said the Princess. 'But one is never so pretty after being mended. Just look at Mr Joker there.'

The Princess was pointing at a very strange-looking clown.

'See,' said the Princess, 'he's fallen over so many times that he has been mended in a hundred places. He has cracks all over him.'

Eventually Dorothy and her friends reached the other side of the village, where they had to climb another wall to get out. This time they stood on the Lion's back and scrambled over the top.

Then the Lion took a long run and jumped

over the wall. But not before his swishing tail had knocked down a china house, a church and a library.

'I'm glad I'm unbreakable,' said the Scarecrow. 'I'd hate to be made of china. There are worse things in the world than being a stuffed Scarecrow.'

They found the path and set off again. Now the travellers entered another forest.

'This forest is perfectly delightful,' said the Lion. 'Never have I seen such a beautiful place.'

'It seems very gloomy to me,' said the Scarecrow.

'Not a bit of it!' replied the Lion. 'I should like to live here all my life. No wild beast such as I could wish for a nicer home.'

That evening they slept under the trees. They were woken the next day by the sound of wild beasts growling.

Dorothy and the others were afraid, but not the Lion.

'We are in no danger,' said the Lion, 'but it sounds to me like the beasts in this forest are in trouble. They need a leader.'

As the Lion spoke, some beasts led by a huge tiger slowly approached him.

'Welcome, oh King of the Forest!' said the tiger. 'You have come just in time to fight our enemy and bring peace to the forest once more.'

'What's the trouble?' asked the Lion, quietly.

'We are all in danger of being eaten by a monster that has come into the forest. It is like a great spider, with a body as big as an elephant. It has eight legs, as long as tree trunks!'

'Are there any lions in the forest?' asked the Lion.

'None,' replied the tiger. 'The monster has eaten them all. But none of them was as large and brave-looking as you.'

The Lion thought for a moment, and then spoke again. 'I will kill your enemy if you bow down to me and obey me as King of the Forest.'

'We'll gladly do that,' said the tiger.

'And where is the monster?' asked the Lion.

'In that oak tree,' replied the tiger, pointing to a nearby tree.

The Lion marched across to the tree. The monster spider was lying asleep when the Lion first saw him.

The creature looked so ugly that Lion turned his nose up in disgust.

Its huge body was covered in rough hair and its great mouth was filled with giant teeth. Yet the strange thing was that the neck joining the creature's head to its enormous body was as thin as a man's wrist.

The Lion didn't hesitate. He knew for sure that it was easier to fight a sleeping beast than one that was wide awake.

So he leapt on the monster, landing on its back. With one blow from his great paw, he knocked the creature's head from its body.

The Lion returned to the other creatures. 'You need not fear your enemy any more,' he said proudly. 'The monster is dead.'

Then the beasts bowed down to the Lion as their King.

'I shall be your King,' said the Lion. 'But first I must see my friend Dorothy safely on her way home. Then I will return to you.'

Chapter 25

The Terrible Hammer Heads

Once out of the forest, the travellers found their path blocked by a great hill of rocks and boulders. They were about to climb over when a voice cried out:

'Keep back. This hill belongs to us, and we don't allow strangers to cross it.'

'Who are you?' shouted the Scarecrow.

A head showed itself above a rock. 'We're called the Hammer Heads,' cried the voice, 'and if you try and cross our hill, you'll find out why.'

'But we must cross it,' said the Scarecrow. 'We're on our way to the country of the Quadlings.'

'You can't cross it,' replied the voice, and out stepped the strangest man the travellers had ever seen.

He was quite short and stout. He had no arms at all, and his neck was a mass of wrinkles.

'I'm sorry,' said the Scarecrow, becoming much bolder when he saw the man had no arms, 'but we must pass over your hill, whether you like it or not. And there's no way you can stop us.'

How wrong he was!

The Scarecrow took one step forward. As quick as lightning, the armless man's head shot forward and knocked him off his feet. It was as if the neck worked on a giant spring.

The Scarecrow tumbled to the ground. 'See!' said the man. 'We may not have arms, but we can fight. We're not called Hammer Heads for nothing.'

A chorus of laughter came from behind some other rocks.

The Lion was very annoyed at the strange creatures. He roared like thunder and dashed up the hill.

Again, a head shot out, and the Lion tumbled down the hill as if he had been hit by a cannon ball.

'How can we fight people with shooting heads?' said the Lion, after he had recovered. 'We must call up the Winged Monkeys to help us over this hill.'

Dorothy agreed. It would be the third and final time she could use the Golden Cap. She put it on and uttered the magic words.

When the Winged Monkeys arrived, she asked them to carry them over the hill.

The Hammer Heads shrieked with anger when they saw what was happening. But even their long necks couldn't reach Dorothy and her friends.

The monkeys dropped them off on the other side of the hill. 'This is the last time you can summon us,' said the King Monkey. 'So goodbye and good luck!'

Dorothy and her friends had now reached the country of the Quadlings.

The Quadlings themselves were short, jolly people. They seemed very good-natured. A Quadling farmer's wife gave them cakes and cookies, and a bowl of milk to refresh them after their journey.

After that, it was only a short walk to the Castle of Glinda. Three young girls in red uniforms met them at the gate.

'Why have you come to the South Country?' asked one of them.

'To see the Good Witch who rules here,' replied Dorothy.

'Give me your name,' said the second girl, 'and we will see if Glinda will allow you in.'

Dorothy gave her name and the girl hurried into the castle. She returned a few minutes later. Dorothy and her friends were to be admitted immediately.

They went inside and the huge castle door slammed shut behind them.

Chapter 26

The Good Witch Glinda

Dorothy and her friends were escorted to the Good Witch Glinda, who was walking in a beautiful garden.

Glinda was beautiful. Her hair was a rich red colour, falling in soft waves down to her shoulders. Her eyes were bright blue.

'What can I do for you, my children?'

Dorothy told the witch her story, from the day the wind first stole her away from Kansas.

'My greatest wish now,' she said, 'is to get back to Kansas as soon as possible.'

Glinda leaned forward and kissed the little girl on the cheek. 'I am sure I can tell you how to get back to Kansas.'

The Witch had one condition. 'If I do this for you,' she said, 'you must give me the Golden Cap.'

'Willingly,' replied Dorothy. 'It is of no use to me now. I have already used up my three requests of the Winged Monkeys.'

Glinda smiled. 'I don't think I will need their help more than three times,' she said mysteriously.

Dorothy gave her the Golden Cap. Then Glinda asked the Scarecrow what he wanted to do next.

'I must return to the Emerald City,' he answered. 'The people there have made me their new ruler. The only thing that worries me is how I'll get over the hill of the Hammer Heads.'

'I shall command the Winged Monkeys to

carry you back,' replied Glinda. 'For it would be a shame to deprive the people of Emerald City of so wonderful a ruler.'

Turning to the Tin Man, she asked him what he would do when Dorothy left.

He leaned on his axe and thought for a moment. 'The Winkies were very kind to me,' he said. 'They wanted me to rule over them when the Wicked Witch died. I should like nothing better than to be their ruler.'

Glinda smiled again. 'Then my second command to the Winged Monkeys will be to carry you safely to the Winkies. I'm sure you will rule them well.'

Then the witch looked at the Lion. 'What's to become of you when Dorothy's gone?' she asked.

'Beyond the land of the Hammer Heads is a big forest,' answered the Lion. 'The beasts there have asked me to be their King. I think I would be very happy being King of the Forest.'

'Then my third command,' said Glinda, 'will be for the Winged Monkeys to carry you back to that forest.'

Dorothy asked Glinda what she would do with the Golden Cap after she had used it three times.

'I shall give it to the King of the Winged Monkeys,' she said. 'Then he and his band will be free forever after. No one will ever be able to summon them again.'

The Scarecrow, the Tin Man and the Lion all thanked the Good Witch of the South.

Now it was time for Glinda to help Dorothy. 'Your red shoes will carry you over the desert,' said Glinda. 'If you had known the power of those shoes, you could have flown back to Kansas the very first day you came to the Land of Oz.'

'But just think,' said the Scarecrow, 'if you had gone back then, I would never have got my brains. I might have spent my whole life in the farmer's field hanging on a pole.'

'And I should never have had my lovely heart,' said the Tin Man. 'I would have stood and rusted away in the forest until the end of the world.'

'And I should have lived as a coward forever,' said the Lion. 'And no beast in the forest would have had a single good word to say about me, let alone ask me to be their King.'

'This is true,' said Dorothy. 'And I am glad to have been useful to my friends. But how will my shoes fly me home?'

'The red shoes,' explained Glinda, 'have wonderful powers. And one of the most curious is that they can carry you to any place in the world. All you have to do is knock your heels together three times and command the shoes to carry you wherever you wish to go.'

Dorothy said a fond farewell to her friends before she left.

She threw her arms around the Lion's neck and kissed him, and patted his head tenderly.

Then she kissed the Tin Man. He was already starting to cry at the thought of losing his friend. Dorothy oiled his joints for him.

Dorothy gave the Scarecrow such a big hug that she almost squeezed out all his stuffing.

Glinda then summoned the Winged Monkeys. 'They'll be waiting for you outside the castle,' she told the group.

Dorothy, Toto and the others walked outside, and saw that seven Winged Monkeys had arrived.

The first three picked up the Lion and carried him away towards the forest.

Dorothy, the Tin Man and the Scarecrow waved to him. The Lion raised a regal paw in return, as he disappeared over the hill of the Hammer Heads.

The next two monkeys carried away the Tin Man. Dorothy and the Scarecrow waved to him as he made his way to the Wicked Witch's Castle to become Ruler of the Winkies.

The last two monkeys picked up the Scarecrow. He waved to Dorothy one last time, as the monkeys carried him into the clouds on his way back to the Emerald City.

Dorothy watched the Scarecrow until he disappeared completely.

Then it was her turn. She took Toto in her arms and followed Glinda's instructions.

She clapped the heels of her shoes together three times and said: 'Take us home to Aunt Em!'

Instantly, she and Toto were whirring through the air, so swiftly that all Dorothy could feel was the wind whistling past her ears. In no time at all she felt a gentle bump as she landed on the ground again.

Chapter 27

Home Again

Dorothy looked up. 'Good gracious!' she cried.

She was sitting on the broad Kansas prairie. And right in front of her was a new house that Uncle Henry must have built after the wind carried away the old one.

Uncle Henry was milking the cows in the barnyard. Toto jumped out of Dorothy's arms and ran towards him, barking furiously.

Dorothy stood up and discovered she was

standing in her bare feet. The red shoes must have fallen off during her flight through the air.

Aunt Em had just come out of the house to water her cabbages, when she looked up and saw Dorothy running towards her.

'My darling child!' she cried, hugging and kissing Dorothy. 'Where in the world have you come from?'

'From the Land of Oz,' replied Dorothy. 'And oh, Aunt Em, I'm so glad to be back home again!'

'From the Land of where?' said Aunt Em who was very confused.

'Never mind for now,' said Dorothy. 'I'll try and explain later.'

***

Dorothy never did manage to explain to Aunt Em and Uncle Henry where she had been. She did not mention the name of Oz again.

She didn't even mention the names of the Scarecrow, the Tin Man or the Lion.

But Dorothy never stopped thinking about them.

She often wondered how the Lion was ruling his new forest kingdom; and what the Tin Man was doing in the Land of the Winkies. She always smiled when she thought of the Scarecrow, King of the Castle, in Emerald City.

She could easily imagine the Lion boasting to his people about how courageous he was.

She could almost hear the Tin Man telling his people how everyone needed a heart so they could be kind to each other.

Dorothy could also imagine the Scarecrow boasting about his extraordinary new brain.

As the years passed, she liked to think that now and then her old friends would meet to talk about old times. And perhaps they would wonder how she was.

But Dorothy also thought a lot about the small balding man who once ruled the Land of Oz.

Where, oh where, had he gone to, the Wonderful Wizard of Oz?

The End